FOXY

and his Naughty Little Sister

First published in hardback in Great Britain by HarperCollins Publishers Ltd in 1997

1 3 5 7 9 10 8 6 4 2
ISBN 0 00 198219 2 (HB)

First published in Picture Lions in 1997
1 3 5 7 9 10 8 6 4 2
ISBN 0 00 664564 X (PB)

Picture Lions is an imprint of the Children's Division, part of HarperCollins Publishers Ltd.
Text and illustrations copyright © Colin and Jacqui Hawkins 1997
The author/illustrators assert the moral right to be identified as the author/illustrators
of the work.
A CIP catalogue record for this title is available from the British Library.
Printed and bound in Hong Kong.

FOXY

and his Naughty Little Sister

Colin and Jacqui Hawkins

Collins

An Imprint of HarperCollinsPublishers

Sometimes Foxy's little sister was naughty, but she didn't mean to be. One day she was playing in the bathroom.

Splish! Splash! Splosh!

There was water everywhere.

"What a mess!" grumbled Foxy,
as he squelched across the floor.
"I'm sorry," said his little sister.
"It was an accident."
It took a long time to mop up.

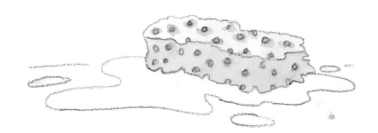

The next day Foxy's little sister played with his kite without asking.

"Whee! This is fun," she laughed, as the kite swooped around the sky.

WHOOSH!

The wind blew the kite high into a
tree where it got tangled up.
"Oh no! Look what you've done!"
cried Foxy.
His kite was torn and broken.
"I'm sorry," said his little sister.
"I didn't mean to do it."

Later that day Foxy could not find
Teddy. He searched everywhere.

"Have you been playing with Teddy?"
Foxy asked his little sister.
"Oh!" she cried. "I think I left him
in the garden."

Quickly Foxy ran to the back door.
There huddled in a soggy heap was
poor Teddy. It was raining and Teddy
was very cold and very wet.

"Look at Teddy," shouted Foxy.
"You're so naughty!"
"I'm sorry," mumbled his little sister.
Poor Teddy!

The next day Foxy's little sister invited
her best friend to play.
Her best friend was
really naughty.

She jumped up and down on the sofa.

BOING!

TWANG!

And she hit Foxy
with a cushion.

BIFF!

She spilt her drink and threw her food.

SPLAT!

She kicked a football through the window.

SMASH!

She broke Foxy's favourite toys.

SNAP!

CRACK!

She scribbled all over the walls.

SCRAWL!

She tore Foxy's comics.

RIP!

And she stuffed toilet rolls down the toilet.

PLOP!

She threw Teddy down
the stairs.

BUMP!
THUMP!

She lifted up her dress and showed her knickers. Then she screamed at the top of her voice.

WHAAAH!

And she never once said sorry.

Foxy and his little sister were so
glad when she went home.
"She's not my best friend any more,"
said Foxy's little sister.
"She's the naughtiest person
I know!"

Foxy grinned at his little sister.
"Perhaps you're not so naughty
after all," he said.

And he meant it.

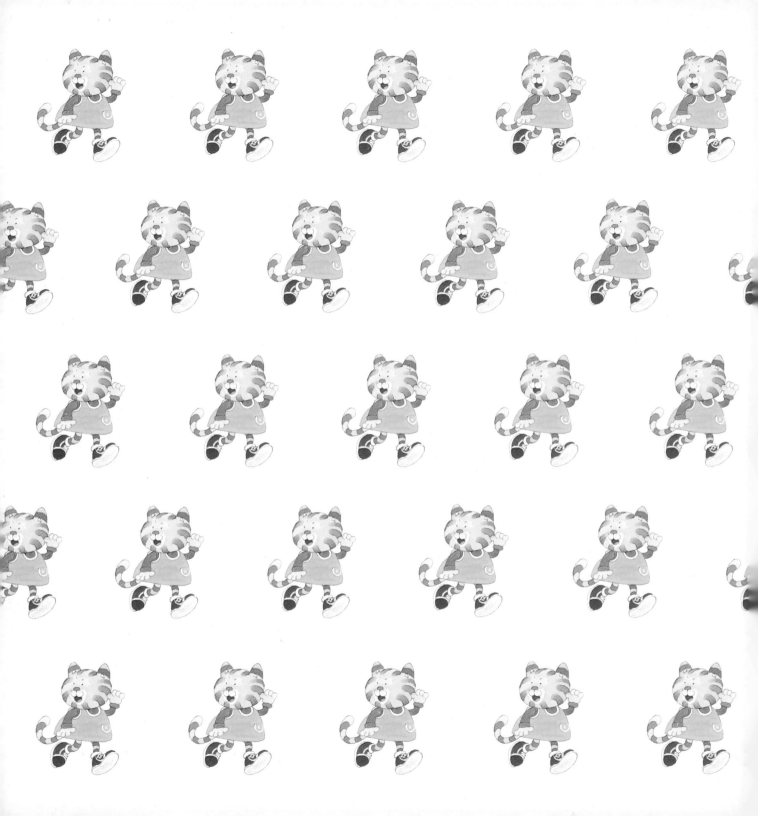

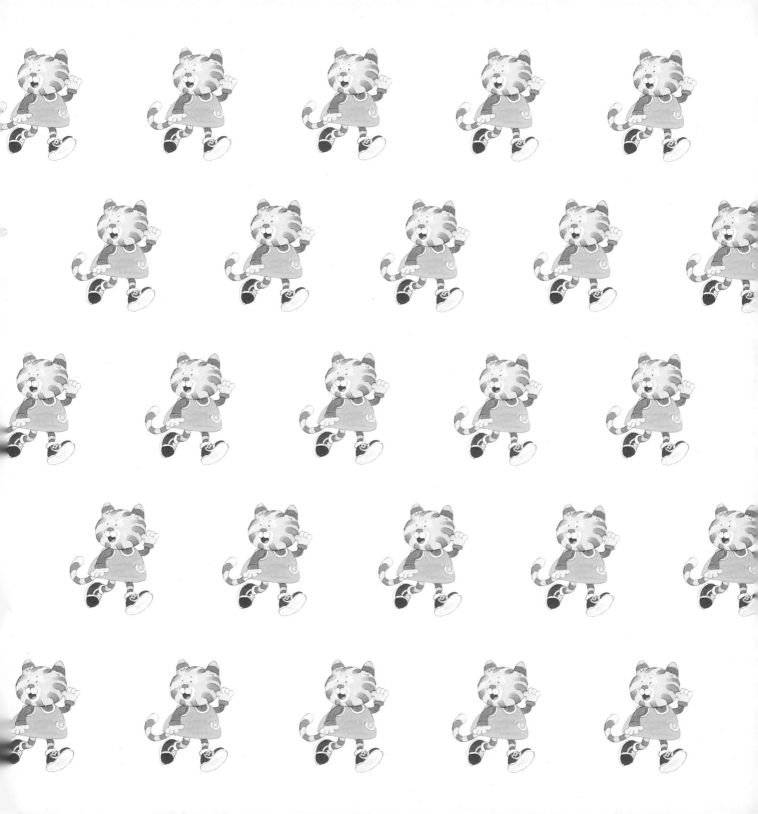

Collect all the stories about Foxy: